FINDING TOLA:
ESCAPING THE HOOD

Vuyo Ngcakani

Vuyo Ngcakani

Finding Tola: Escaping The Hood is a novel, a work of fiction, and a product of the author's imagination. Any resemblance to actual events or persons, living or dead, is entirely coincidental.

For my parents. Thank you for everything.

Vuyo Ngcakani

Chapter 1

It was a successful hunt. Tola Matthews and his friends, Balisa Kamala and Zach Mzi, each carried springboks on their shoulders, as they returned gleefully to their village of Dlambona.

"Patience comes with its rewards, doesn't it, boys?" said Balisa.

The hunt was challenging. The 15-year-old chums had left Dlambona at 5 am and returned at 8 pm. It was the first time they had hunted without older company. First, Zach forgot his water skin, so they had to ration what little water they had. Second, it was the hottest day of the year, with March temperatures soaring to 40°C. Third, many watering holes had dried up, forcing animals to travel distances to find water, and consequently, the hunters ventured far to locate them. Usually, the hunt lasted six hours, not fifteen.

"What took you boys so long?" yelled Thabo.

It wasn't the welcome Tola had expected from his dad.

"Sorry, Tata," he said. "The hunt took longer than expected, but look at what we have."

"Boys, next time, turn around and come home sooner. Your mamas were frantic, and I don't like dealing with that. Drop those animals and go hug your mothers."

Later that evening, the friends hung and bled their kill. They watched the blood drip into metal buckets while seated on a wooden bench. Ukopha was an area on the outskirts of the village where the bloodletting occurred. The hot night air allowed the smell of the carcasses to linger.

"I like the smell of raw meat at night," said Zach.

"You're a sick man, my friend," said Balisa, and they all laughed.

"Mama said it's going to be a while before I go hunting again," said Zach.

Balisa shrugged. "She just said that because she's scared. We're men. We don't need our mamas' permission to do anything."

Tola cast him a glance. "The inkankatha cut off more than your foreskin, my friend."

The friends had grown close as they took the rite of passage into manhood together a couple of years ago. The memory of the pain that shot through Tola when the circumcision occurred made him shudder.

Tola continued, "You would never go against Aunty Ethel's wishes."

Balisa agreed. "I was just kidding. There's no one I fear more than my mother. I'd sooner lock myself in a room with a thousand bees."

The boys gutted their animals and carried the meat to one of the three smoking rooms in the village. These were round mud huts with wooden rods meeting at the apex of the roof. Acacia wood chips lined the floor, and when lit, the smoke filled the hut, infusing the meat with a mouth-watering flavour. After slicing and salting the meat, the friends laid the pieces on a metal rack, and hung the skins out to dry.

"Well, men, it's been a long day, and I'm tired," Tola said. "I can't wait until tomorrow when we smoke our kill. Let's meet here at seven."

Before heading to bed, Tola kissed his mother goodnight and gave his father an appreciative nod. The floored mattress was a welcome sight, and he fell into it fully clothed, forgetting to say his bedtime prayer.

He met Balisa and Zach early the next morning outside the smoke room. They didn't look happy.

"What's wrong?" he asked.

"Did you move our meat?" yelled Balisa.

"What are you talking about?" Tola replied.

His friends led him into the smoke room. While the springbok skins still hung in their place, the smoke racks were bare.

Chapter 2

"Are you okay, son?" asked Jalisa, Tola's mama.

Tola plopped into one of the six chairs surrounding the kitchen table. Jalisa, Thabo, and his seven-year-old sister, Lindi, occupied three other chairs. His three-year-old sister, Nomsa, played outside. Their home resembled others in the village: straw-roofed and round. Jalisa used fabric to separate areas within the dwelling. The clay-built houses kept the interior cool during scorching summer days.

He dropped his head into his hands and sighed deeply. Tola wasn't ignoring his mama; he just didn't want to answer her question. He wasn't okay, but he wasn't sure how to articulate his feelings. His emotions were jumbled: anger, frustration, sadness, violation, and powerlessness. It was as if a ghost had taken their meat, leaving no clues or tracks to follow.

"Tata, has anything like this happened before?" he asked.

"It probably has, Tola. Raids were pretty common back in the day. Recently, the Gamba had a notorious reputation."

"Yes, but they usually let you know they were present. This was done in the dead of night. They slipped in like a breeze and disappeared like a puff of smoke. Who acts like that?"

"I don't know, my son. But I may know someone who can help us find out."

"Who's that?"

"Bwana."

Chapter 3

Tola last saw Bwana two years ago when he attended his rite of passage ceremony. Bwana worked for Ilanga Intelligence and informed Tola that they kept an eye on him because he had demonstrated courage and skill on various occasions. Thabo was with his son at the time and was disturbed that Intelligence would spy on his thirteen-year-old boy. Since then, Bwana had become a friend.

Tola grimaced. "Are you sure we should involve the country's Intelligence in our village affairs?"

"No," said Thabo. "But he may have insights into how to start your investigation."

Jalisa and Tola shared a quizzical glance.

"You are going to investigate this, right?" asked Thabo. "You must find out who stole your meat and hold them accountable."

"Are you serious?" Tola replied. "I was going to chalk it up to a lesson learned and plan my next hunting trip."

Thabo stood up and pushed his chair in. "You could do that," he said. "Or you could seek justice. I have to go back to Lobani. Give Bwana a call. I'm sure he'll have some tips on how to get started."

Lobani was the city where Thabo worked as a domestic servant for the Bukani family. It was about a seven-hour drive from Dlambona. Thabo had worked for the Bukanis for about nine years, and just last year he purchased a car that allowed him to come home more often. Before that, it was months before they saw him again as the bus trip was lengthy, and involved a long journey on foot.

"I thought I was supposed to love my enemies, pray for them, and leave justice to the Lord," said Tola.

"You're to leave vengeance to the Lord."

"Aren't you splitting hairs? That's a distinction without a difference."

"And you're getting too smart for your own good," Thabo replied with a smile. "Come, let's pray. We'll let Jesus decide."

Tola was on board with that idea. Jalisa called Nomsa, and the family held hands.

Tola prayed, "Father, thank you for the favour you have bestowed on this family. We are a loving, healthy family and we give you all the glory. Continue to guide us in everything we do. We pray for a pleasant and safe journey for Tata and for continued success in all that he does. We pray that for all of us. Let me know if I should pursue justice for the stolen springbok, and if so, how to proceed. Thank you for being our God. In Jesus' name, amen."

No sooner had he finished praying than a shadow dimmed the light entering the room. They all looked to see what was blocking the sun's rays.

"Hello, everyone. What's for breakfast?" Bwana inquired, his teeth gleaming

Chapter 4

Everyone enjoyed a bowl of mealie meal porridge. Bwana had a second bowl and expressed his appreciation for Jalisa's hospitality.

"I'm sure you're wondering why I'm here," he said, reaching for a cup of coffee.

Their silence encouraged him to continue.

"We have reason to believe that the bandits calling themselves The Future may be reassembling. I thought you should know, given your history with them."

Tola stiffened. The Future was a group of so-called liberators whose aim was to overthrow the government of Ilanga and rule on their terms. They would 'recruit' teenage boys, drug them, train them to use weapons, and use them to raid villages and kidnap other boys.

Three years ago, when Tola lived in Lobani, the school football team was on its way to a match when a faction of The Future stopped them, herded the boys into trucks, and took them to a camp deep in the forest. Their goal was to build an army of brainwashed boys who would grow into men obedient to their leader, whose name was Jogba.

The thought of him sent Tola's heart racing. He was a charismatic leader who delivered inspirational speeches and flattering words, but he was an evil man who filled his recruits with drugs and lies. Looking into his eyes felt like staring into the eyes of the devil. Thankfully, Tola and two of his friends escaped and found help. Jogba was never caught, but many of his followers were arrested, and the boys were returned to their parents.

"What makes you think The Future is regrouping?" asked Thabo.

"From the information we've gathered. We have spies in many of these dissident groups. With the country's elections coming up next year, there is an increase in rhetoric regarding change needed in government. We may see The Future form a political party in some capacity."

"Can they do that?" asked Tola.

"They can, but not in their current form. And Jogba can't run; he has a warrant for his arrest, so if he shows his face, he will stand trial for his crimes. However, he can still pull strings while in hiding."

"I have to go," said Thabo, standing up from the table. "We will be vigilant, but let's not forget who we have on our side. Jesus helped you escape The Future and will protect you from their clutches again."

"You're right, Tata," said Tola, nodding and breathing a little easier. He had forgotten how the Lord had seen him through it all.

"Of course, I'm right," said Thabo, as he put on his favourite blue denim jacket. "Now we have Bwana right here in our kitchen. Let's see if he can help you solve the mystery of the missing meat."

Chapter 5

Jalisa decided that she and Nomsa would walk Lindi to school and then join the other mothers at the park. Tola, accompanied by Balisa and Zach, took Bwana to Ukopha, where the crime occurred. The numerous footprints outside the hut were of no use, as they belonged to the three friends. Upon entering the hut, Bwana was impressed by the three hanging springbok skins.

"Any chance I could buy one of those skins?" he asked.

The friends exchanged glances.

"Those were our first kills on our first hunt together," said Tola. "They are sentimental trophies. I'll get one for you next time. It's going to happen sooner than we intended."

"Okay," said Bwana.

He walked around the edge of the hut, careful not to add his shoe prints to the mix. His eyes surveyed the room, but he was hard to read. Was his silence an indication that he didn't see anything, or was he concentrating and assimilating all the information first? Eventually, he looked at them and pointed up.

"That's the only way they could have made it in," he said.

The hut had four small holes in the roof to allow for smoke to escape.

"No man can fit through those openings," said Tola.

"No, but a child could," observed Bwana.

He led them outside.

"That tree was the means."

Bwana indicated a tall baobab tree that grew a few feet from the wall of the hut. A single branch stretched far enough to allow someone to drop onto the roof.

"Someone could lower a child down with a rope and pull them up once they secured the meat. They probably did it a few times but it wouldn't take long. It could have been two men lowering and raising the child. I believe that's how they did it."

Tola looked at his friends stunned. They had just brought in the kill last night. Was it an inside job? Surely not.

"Okay, we know how they did it," said Balisa, "but who did it?"

The question hung there for a bit. Tola wanted to ask about using satellite images but thought that would be ridiculous.

"How about satellite imagery?" Balisa asked excitedly. "I've seen them used by the CIA in movies. You have access to that, right?"

Tola felt like slapping him.

Bwana smiled. "Accessing satellite images for a meat heist is a gross misuse of government resources. If you want to find out who the thieves are, you'll have to do some real investigative work. You need to interview witnesses."

"It was done in the middle of the night," said Zach. "There are no witnesses."

"There are no eyewitnesses. One thing I've learned about thieves is that they like to brag. Keep an ear out for that. Someone may have come into some extra meat and is having a party. I have to go. Good luck."

Tola walked Bwana to his car.

"You could have called and told us about The Future," Tola said. "Why did you drive all this way?"

"It's been two years since we've talked, Tola, and I wanted to see how you were doing. Are you happy you returned to Dlambona?"

"Ecstatic," replied Tola. "I miss my friends in Lobani, but the pull of home was strong for all of us. We had to come back."

Bwana nodded. "Home is where the heart is, as they say." He placed a hand on Tola's shoulder. "You continue to impress us, young man. You're growing tall and strong. How tall are you now?"

"Almost six feet."

"Impressive. And exciting."

"Why?" asked Tola. "When will you tell me more about your interest in me?"

"Soon, Tola. Very soon."

With a handshake, he entered his car and drove off. Tola watched as the dust settled and the car disappeared around a bend.

Chapter 6

Tola returned to his friends. "Well, men, it's 9 am. If we run, we can make it to second period. Let's grab our satchels and go."

The Villages High School was a thirty-five-minute walk from Dlambona, but they made it in twelve minutes. The school was named for the students it served, coming from several villages, near and far. They arrived just in time for Tola's favourite class: Civics.

Ilanga had four government structures: National, Provincial, City, and Township. Townships were governed by Chiefs and comprised a certain number of villages, each overseen by an Elder. As a boy, Tola would sit within earshot of adults discussing politics. Through these conversations, he learned about his country's history, he understood why the discussions were often heated. People were divided along many lines, including tribal, religious, and gender. He appreciated that in the end, everyone parted as friends.

But that wasn't the reason he liked Civics. Her name was Pumla, and this was the only class they had together. Her skin was as dark as panga panga wood, as smooth as Lake Sibayi on a windless day, and as soft as wool on a lamb-at least, it looked that soft. She lived in the village of Madiba, a twenty-minute easy jog north of Dlambona. Her smile brightened his day, and when she asked him for a pencil sharpener, his hand shook.

The teacher, Mr. Kimani, was speaking. Tola knew him well as Mr. Kimani was also the football coach and Tola played on the senior team.

"You and your partner have four weeks to complete your assigned project," said Mr. Kimani. "I will hand out your topics; your partner is the person with the same topic as you. You have to find each other. I know who has which topic, so you can't change partners. Go."

Tola didn't feel like walking around.

"Who has The History of the Ilanga Provinces?" he asked.

"I do."

Tola turned to see Pumla walking toward him.

Chapter 7

The rest of the school day was a blur for Tola. He was called out in one class for daydreaming and in another for not paying attention. Balisa and Zach ran home after school, but Tola preferred to walk. How was he going to work with Pumla on this project? Just thinking about it quickened his heart.

"Would Tata be in his quarters right now?" he asked Jalisa as he walked through the door.

"Hello, son. How was school today?"

"Sorry, Mama," said Tola sheepishly. "School was fine."

He planted a kiss on her cheek.

"It's 4 o'clock, so he might be," said Jalisa. "Why?"

"I want to talk to him about something. It's man stuff."

"Okay," said Jalisa, smiling. "I'll give you some privacy."

She waited for Tola to make the phone call and ensured he and his father connected.

"Hello, Tata. How was your drive?"

"Smooth sailing, son. How was your talk with Bwana?"

They continued with small talk until there was a short silence.

"There's a reason I called," said Tola.

"Go ahead, son."

"When did you know that Mama was the one?"

Thabo laughed knowingly. "What's her name?"

"Pumla Zizi," Tola replied. "Every time I see her, my heart races and my palms get clammy. Now we've been partnered for a school project. What am I going to do?"

"My dearest son, you're caught up in one of life's contradictions. You've fought men and beasts with unrivalled bravery but it is a woman who brings you to your knees. Have you told your mama?"

"No," answered Tola. "I thought you could give me some words of wisdom."

"Son, I could offer advice but each woman is different. I can't tell you to do this or that. What I can tell you is to be yourself. You've been paired for the project so focus on that. What is it about?"

"We have to give a presentation on the history of Ilanga provinces."

"That's an interesting topic. Make sure you've studied it before meeting with Pumla. When you're brainstorming ideas, be sure to listen. Don't try to show her that you know it all because you don't. This isn't new to you, son. Your mama and I have drilled this into you already, and I've seen you put it into practice. The only difference now is that there's a young lady you like in front of you. Trust me. Talk to Mama. She can give you some pointers."

Tola took a deep breath. "Okay, I will."

He didn't get another word out before the door swung open and Lindi walked in, followed by Jalisa, who was seething.

"Give your sister the phone so she can explain to her father what happened at school today," said Jalisa.

Tola slowly handed Lindi the phone and gave her a quizzical look. She didn't respond.

"Read your father this note," said Jalisa.

"Hello, Tata," said Lindi.

"Read, Lindiwe," said Thabo, using her full name when portraying seriousness.

"Dear Mr. and Mrs. Matthews,

Your daughter was involved in a fight today with a boy in her class. As you know, fighting is unacceptable in our school, and as a result, Lindi Matthews has been suspended until a parent meets with us to discuss the matter. Please call the office to set up an appointment.

Mrs. Patricia Dambe

Headmistress

"This is not like you, Lindi," said Thabo. "What happened?"

Lindi said nothing.

"Lindiwe, what happened?"

A tear escaped her left eye. She wiped it away, annoyed that it had happened. Tola had never seen his sister this defiant. A knock on the door broke the silence, and a woman peeked in. Upon seeing Lindi, she glared.

"Hello," said Jalisa. "Can we help you?"

"My name is Gladys, and this is my son, Terence."

Gladys beckoned behind her, and a boy approached sheepishly. His face was swollen, and there were welts on his arms. His clothing was dusty, as if he had been rolling on the ground. His eyes were bloodshot from crying.

"I wanted you to see what your daughter did," said Gladys.

Tola was surprised by her demeanour. Gladys wasn't angry; she was unusually calm given the circumstances. He couldn't imagine his mama acting similarly if the roles were reversed. He was even more surprised that Lindi was being accused of inflicting this beating on Terence. He took the phone from his sister.

"Tata, can I call you back? Someone is here."

"Sure, son. I'll be here."

"Aunt Gladys, do you expect us to believe that my little sister did this to your son?" he asked, hanging up.

Gladys continued to face Jalisa. "I'm taking my son to see the doctor. I want to make sure that there is no permanent damage to his face. I have one question: Why are you teaching your daughter intonga?"

Intonga is an ancient African art of stick fighting, one of the battle skills taught to boys of the Dlamini tribe.

"What?" Jalisa responded, perplexed. "Lindi has not learned the art of stick fighting. What gives you that idea?"

"Do you think she injured my son with her fists? Speaking with Terence and other witnesses, Lindi showed remarkable skill for someone so young. There's no way she taught herself. I ask again: why are you teaching her a skill we reserve for older boys, not young girls?"

Tola caught his sister's eye. He expected her to look away, but she maintained her gaze. He gave her a quizzical look, and her expression gave him the answer: she was indeed culpable for Terence's injuries. He mouthed 'How?' and Jalisa noticed.

"Tola, what do you know about this? Have you been teaching your sister intonga?"

It was fitting that Jalisa would ask Tola that question as he was an expert stick fighter who had won many battles, some against much older opponents.

"No, I haven't, Mama," Tola replied. "I think Lindi has some explaining to do."

"Lindiwe," Jalisa said, sharply. "Speak!"

Lindi swallowed. "He deserved it," she said.

"Why?" asked Jalisa.

"He knows who took your meat and wouldn't tell me," said Lindi, scowling at Terence.

Tola turned to Terence.

"Is it true? Do you know who took my meat?" he asked.

"Don't answer that," Gladys interjected. "Let's go." At the door, she turned and added, "You'd better rein in that daughter of yours. She's dangerous."

Chapter 8

"Once again, what happened, Lindiwe?" Thabo asked loudly.

Tola held the phone receiver so Lindi and his mama could hear him. The three of them sat at the kitchen table.

Lindi glanced at Tola, who gestured toward the phone with his head. He smiled to reassure her.

"I did what you taught me, Tata. You told me to stand up to bullies."

"Terence bullied you?" asked Tata.

Lindi nodded, though her father couldn't see it. "He came up to me and pushed me down. Then he said he heard that my brother lost some meat and he wanted me to tell him that it tasted delicious."

Tola squeezed the receiver and gnashed his teeth. It had been the toughest hunt he had been on, so the reward was satisfying and he looked forward to savouring the springbok.

Lindi continued, "I demanded he tell me who stole the meat. He said, "Make me!" So I did."

Tola imagined the look on his father's face, which had to be the same as his mother's, mirroring his shock. Their jaws dropped, eyes wide, and heads leaning forward in disbelief.

"What do you mean you made him?" asked Tola. "You said he wouldn't tell you?"

"I'm not interested in that," Tata interjected. "We know why. I want to know how. What's this I heard about you and intonga? Is it true?"

Lindi hesitated. Her teacher had sworn her to secrecy, and she didn't want to break that confidence. She also knew she couldn't lie to her parents.

"I have been learning, Tata," she said. "Please don't ask me who my teacher is. She doesn't want to be revealed."

"She?" asked Tola.

"Yes, she!" Lindi replied. "Do you think only males can stick fight?"

Tola was reminded of his battle with Yoliswa. She was a few years older than him but highly skilled. Her village of Shanla taught both males and females the art of intonga, which was unusual.

"We're not going to ask you to break someone's confidence, Lindi," said Thabo. "But I want to meet your teacher. You are not to see her again until I return next week. Is that understood?"

"Yes, Tata," said Lindi.

"It sounds like you did defend yourself, so we'll let this one go. In the future, don't be quick to strike. With great skill comes great responsibility. I'm sure your teacher will tell you the same thing."

"Okay, Tata," said Lindi.

"Tola, forget about the meat, my son. I don't want you to pursue this mystery. Chalk it up to an experience and look forward to your next hunting trip. Deal?"

Tola's expression indicated that was what he had wanted to do in the first place.

"Yes, Tata."

"Good." He sighed deeply. "This news will travel fast and we're going to hear from Elder Marikana and will have to meet with the council and give an explanation for our daughter learning intonga. Those men are traditionalists, so I know it won't go well. I love you all. Goodnight."

Chapter 9

Tola tried to get Lindi to divulge the name of her teacher, but she stood firm. His money was on Yoliswa but he didn't press her. His thoughts turned to Pumla. He thought God had a sense of humour by partnering him with the young lady who made him stammer and his heart gallop.

He knew a little about the Ilanga provinces but a visit to the school library was a must. He arrived at school early the next day to get a head start.

"Great minds think alike."

Tola looked up from the table to see Pumla smiling at him. He had never seen such gleaming white teeth and hair that shimmered in the fluorescent light.

"I guess they do," he said, gathering himself. "I've got some books here that we can look at together if you'd like."

Pumla leafed through one of the books. "How about we each take four provinces, learn what we can, and write down some ideas? We can meet in a week to see how we're doing. What do you think?"

"That sounds like a great idea," said Tola. Anything she suggested would have seemed great to him. He enjoyed watching her lips move. "Which four do you want?"

Tola decided which books would best assist him with the four provinces he had selected and checked them out of the library. There was no civics today, so he wouldn't see Pumla in a classroom setting. He might at lunchtime, though. He ran into Zach and Balisa in first class which was English.

"Hello, loverboy," said Balisa, slapping Tola's back. "What's this we hear about Lindi stick-handling a boy?"

"Stick-handling?" asked Tola, amused.

"We heard you had a visit from the lad's mom," said Zach. "What happened?"

"How did you hear about that?" asked Tola.

"It's all over the village," said Zach.

That was one advantage of living in the city over village life. In the city, family affairs remained private for the most part. In Dlambona, privacy was practically impossible.

"I'll tell you later," Tola said. "We need to decide when we're going hunting again. The sooner, the better."

"So we're not going to investigate the criminals who stole our first kill?" asked Zach.

Tola shrugged. "Tata wants me to forget about it, so I will."

His friends eye him expectedly.

"For now," Tola added.

Then the English teacher walked in.

Chapter 10

Lindi whacked her imaginary opponent as she sparred with a single stick. Her rod sliced through the air with precision, striking the imaginary left knee, and then landing on the phantom left temple. She stood over her foe victoriously. A pair of hands applauded.

"Well done, Lindi. Your progress has been meteoric, my child."

Lindi beamed as she always did whenever Yoliswa complimented her.

"Sit down, Lindi. I want to talk to you."

Lindi glanced at her watch and saw that it was a little past 11:00 am. This was how she spent recess every week. After the bell, she would run for ten minutes to a clearing Yoliswa had created after approaching her a few months ago. Lindi was self-taught in the art of intonga, having watched the boys practice, and followed their movements in the shadows. Yoliswa spotted her and recognized her raw talent. After learning that Lindi was from Dlambona and was Tola's sister, Yoliswa agreed to take her on as a student for a while. They sat down, cross-legged, on the dusty ground.

"I need to speak to your parents, Lindi."

This surprised but pleased Lindi. She wasn't sure if Yoliswa would be willing to meet with her Mama and Tata.

"How's this Saturday?" she asked.

"What?"

Lindi opened up about what had transpired at school with Terence and the following events at home.

"My dad would like to meet you, and he's home on Saturday. Are you able to come?"

"Is Uncle Thabo angry that we went behind his back with your training?" asked Yoliswa after a beat.

"I'm sure the deception will come up," answered Lindi.

Yoliswa nodded. "He's going to be disappointed in me. That's what I dread the most. I respect your father, and he might feel that I betrayed him."

Lindi rose and hugged her teacher. The meeting was over, and she had to return to school. Yoliswa confirmed she would be at the house on Saturday morning. Lindi picked up her stick and sprinted to her next class.

Chapter 11

"Are you nervous?" asked Tola.

"A little," replied Lindi.

Tola looked at his little sister and shook his head. They had just cleared the table of breakfast dishes and were waiting for Yoliswa's arrival. It was a warm, sunny morning and Thabo and Jalisa had gone for a walk with Nomsa.

"I feel like you skipped your childhood," he said.

"What do you mean?" Lindi asked.

"You're seven years old, right?"

"Yes."

"Well, seven-year-olds aren't supposed to act like you."

Lindi laughed. "How are they supposed to act?"

Tola shrugged. "I don't know. Not like you."

"I'm still your little sister, big brother. That will never change."

Tola felt a twinge of sadness because things had changed, and he had nothing to do with it. He wasn't upset that his little sister could defend herself; of that he was proud. He wasn't the one who taught her what she knew. Truthfully, if she had come to him, he would have declined. It wasn't the Dlamini way to teach girls the art of stick fighting, and he wasn't one to go against tradition. She was.

The early walkers returned and Yoliswa was with them. Jalisa busied herself making tea and magwinya while Tola helped her, leaving Thabo, Yoliswa, and Lindi to talk.

"Yoliswa," Thabo began, "I respect the Shanla clan and appreciate that they teach females the art of stick fighting. But that is not the Dlamini way. The fact that you are teaching our seven-year-old daughter without our permission is unconscionable. How do you justify your actions?"

Wow, Tata is going for the jugular and not mincing words, thought Tola. He and his mama usually chatted freely when he helped her in the kitchen, but this morning was silent. Even the lowing of cattle and the clucking of hens were muted.

"Sir, you are right," said Yoliswa. "I should have sought your approval before agreeing to train Lindi. Would you have given it to me?"

Yoliswa locked eyes with Thabo as she spoke, not defiant but fearless.

"We'll never know now, will we?" Thabo replied. "How did you meet?"

"I saw her practicing by herself while I went for a run. Her technique was good, but she was obviously untrained. I intended to give her some pointers, but it developed into full training sessions. If it makes any difference, I wasn't going to have any more lessons until I had spoken to you. That was before you requested this meeting."

"It makes no difference," said Thabo, curtly. "Lindi, what is this about practicing? I don't understand."

Tola and his mama brought the tea and magwinya cakes to the table.

Lindi cleared her throat. "Since I was about four years old, I watched the boys go through the motions of learning intonga. I had my own sticks and fought my shadow, practicing every day whenever I could. I'm really good, Tata. Please don't make me stop."

"She is outstanding," said Yoliswa, earning a glare from Thabo.

"What you've neglected to teach her, Yoliswa, is the responsibility that comes with acquiring these skills. Sometimes, walking away is the better option. Not every challenge needs to be met with violence."

Tola thought he saw his father's eyes moistening but maybe it was his own.

"Things are changing so fast," said Thabo. "I long for the simple days when everything was clear and everyone knew their place in the world. Thank you for coming by, Yoliswa. My wife and I will come to a decision. You're welcome to stay and enjoy some magwinya."

The meeting was over. Thabo stood up and walked out. Tola followed him.

Chapter 12

Tola hurried to keep pace with his dad. It was only mid-morning, but the day had the brightness of noon. The sky stretched wide and cloudless, the kind of blue that seemed endless. Birds darted from the trees, and somewhere nearby, a rooster crowed again as if it hadn't already declared the morning twice before.

"Tata," he said, "you left so quickly. What are you thinking?"

Thabo didn't answer right away. He rubbed his brow, squinting against the sunlight. For a moment, Tola thought he might not speak at all. Then, slowly, the words came out, heavy and unexpected.

"I'm thinking of my sister," Tata said. His voice was quieter than usual, almost fragile. "She once begged my father to teach her intonga. He refused. She died young and defenseless, during a raid. And I still wonder, if she had known how to fight, would she be alive today?"

Tola froze mid-step. He had never heard this

story. His father always seemed unshakable, but now, Tola saw pain and worry worn into the lines of his face.

"Then why stop Lindi?" Tola asked quietly. "Doesn't that prove she should learn?"

Tata shook his head. His jaw worked, but his eyes gave him away. "Because the memory of that loss blinds me. I fear both paths: teaching her or forbidding her. Either way can lead to regret."

They stopped at the fence line, where the posts threw dark lines across the sunlit yard. Goats bleated from a pen. Women's voices floated on the morning air. Life carried on around them, yet it felt to Tola as if the world had stilled for this moment.

"Tata, I thought you were certain about everything," Tola said, his own voice trembling.

A small smile touched his father's mouth, a smile full of sorrow and affection at once. "No, my son. Certainty is for the young. Fatherhood is walking each day with choices you pray will not crush your children."

The words struck Tola deep. He looked at his father, not as the invincible man he had always known, but as a man who carried burdens no one else could see. And somehow, that made him respect him more.

"Maybe it's not about right or wrong," Tola whispered. "Maybe it's about walking with her, so she doesn't carry it alone."

Tata turned to him fully then, his eyes no longer shadowed but shining in the morning light. He pulled Tola close, his embrace firm and warm.

"You remind me that I am not alone either," Tata said, his voice steadier now. "Thank you, Tola."

Tola embraced his father back. "You're welcome, Tata," he said.

Chapter 13

On Monday, Tola went to school early to complete his part of the project he had with Pumla. His second period was Civics, so he wanted to ensure his part was done. Not much had been said to him regarding the Lindi situation and he didn't inquire about his parents' plans. Mama tried in vain to relieve the tension in the house. By the time Tata left for his job, his parents had not decided on the Lindi matter. Tola sensed that they had come to a conclusion but were letting Lindi sweat it out as a form of punishment.

"Good morning, Tola," said Balisa.

Tola looked up to see his friends with sullen expressions on their faces.

"What's wrong?" he asked.

"Are you serious," Zach replied, noticing the history books on the table. "We waited for you, as we do every Monday, to come to school together. This fascination with Pumla has you distracted. Did you even hear the bell for first class?"

"No," said Tola, clamouring to his feet and knocking over the chair. "I'm sorry, guys. Let's go."

The truth was he had forgotten, which was unlike him. It wasn't just the project with Pumla; the meeting with Yoliswa and its impact on his family also weighed heavily on his mind. It had been an eventful weekend, one that had excluded his friends, which was unusual.

Pumla wasn't in Civics class. Tola discovered that she hadn't been in the first period either. I wonder if she's sick, he thought. He would have to connect with her tomorrow. The next Civics class was on Wednesday but he'd seek her out at recess.

She wasn't at school the next day or Wednesday. Tola approached the Civics teacher and suggested they might need an extension as Pumla had been absent.

"Pumla came down with a severe cold," said Mr. Kimani. "She is feeling better, but her parents decided to keep her home this week. Why don't you give her a call and see if she's up for visitors? Check with her parents first, of course."

The thought never crossed Tola's mind, and the idea of going to her house was daunting. Mr. Kimani saw the dread on his face and laughed.

"Tola, you have three weeks to complete the project, which is plenty of time for smart students like you and Pumla. Relax. She'll be back next week and you can collaborate again. Okay?"

Tola nodded.

Chapter 14

The predicted meeting with the Dlamini council took place the following Saturday morning. Thabo returned home late on Friday night to ensure he was available for it. The meeting occurred under a massive Jacaranda tree in a clearing called The Meeting Place. Elder Marikana sat between six councillors, three men on either side of him. Many villagers attended along with some from other villages in the township. Others thought that the meeting was a waste of time claiming that the situation could be resolved with Marikana paying a visit to the Matthews home.

Children weren't allowed at council meetings, so Lindi stayed home with Nomsa. Thabo and Jalisa were relieved that Lindi wouldn't have to defend herself. Tola did not sit with his parents but stood nearby with Zach and Balisa.

"It's a large turnout, isn't it, Tola?" said Balisa. "Your family is always in the middle of something, my friend."

"What are you talking about?" asked Tola.

"Your adventures with Jogba are legendary. Why can't you keep a low profile?"

Tola didn't answer because the meeting was called to order with the blow of a ram's horn. Tola's heart began racing and he glanced at his parents to see how they were doing. Both were stoic but Mom leaned in closer to Dad.

Elder Marikana had a reputation of being a fair man. He smiled fondly at Thabo and Jalisa who were about ten years his senior.

"Good morning, uncle and auntie," he began, addressing them respectfully. "I know this meeting was called suddenly and that some deem it unnecessary. I disagree and this is why?" He leaned forward. "We are the Dlamini and we have traditions that set us apart from other tribes. One of them is that we do not teach our females about the use of combat weapons or techniques. This has worked well for us throughout the centuries and we see no reason to change now."

Maybe we should, thought Tola.

"How do you feel about the tradition?" asked Marikana. "Do you believe it is old-fashioned and that we should enter the modern era by including females in combat?"

Thabo cleared his throat before responding. "It is old-fashioned, Elder, but we have no issue with the tradition."

"Good, because the worst thing someone can do is change something just because it fits in with the times. Would you agree with that?"

Thabo smiled. "I wouldn't say it's the worst thing but it isn't wise. Culture is important to one's identity."

"Yes, it is," said Marikana. "So, you agree then that Lindi will cease her training immediately and stop opposing our tradition."

Thabo and Jalisa exchanged glances.

"I would like permission to speak," said Jalisa.

Marikana looked to his councillors for consensus. All agreed, which was no surprise, as Jalisa was a respected woman in the village.

Jalisa stood up and spoke loud enough to be heard by everyone. She wasn't only addressing the council; she was engaging with the audience.

"Elder Marikana and councilmen, my husband and I have two daughters, and we are raising them to be independent and courageous. Are you aware of the incident that led to the discovery of Lindi's skills?"

The council nodded.

"She was responding to a bully. We don't approve of her methods, but she was defending herself. There are two lessons we can glean from her actions. One: she can defend herself. How many women have found themselves in a frightening situation, where they have been assaulted by a man and couldn't escape?"

Many ladies lifted their hands and "me's" and "yes's" were heard.

"And two: she had the confidence to use her skills. If you have the know-how but are fearful, then what's the point?"

"I'm still waiting to hear your point, Auntie," said Marikana.

"Here's my point, Elder. We agree that only men should go into battle with our enemies. But why can't we teach our women to defend themselves? Why can't we teach them to use intonga as a means of fighting back and giving them a chance to escape or survive?"

The Meeting Place buzzed like excited African bees. Some could be heard agreeing with Jalisa and others disagreed.

"Your mama is one brave lady," said Zach.

Indeed, thought Tola, beaming with pride. When Mama spoke, people listened. He was proud of her. He agreed that girls should be taught how to defend themselves. It wasn't often that a man accompanied them to draw water from the river or trips to the market, and many had returned having suffered harm. But he wasn't sure that teaching stick-fighting to females was the answer. Not because they weren't capable-his bout with Yoliswa was proof of that. He felt that it might be a distraction having girls train with the boys and the boys might take it easy on them. Teaching the females self-defence would be more practical.

"Tola!"

Hearing his name pulled Tola out of his contemplation. He wasn't sure who called him so he looked at Tata in case it was him. Tata nodded his head toward Elder Marikana.

"Yes, Elder?" Tola answered, bewildered. He had never been acknowledged at these meetings.

"What's your opinion? Does your Mama make a good point?"

Tola swallowed, but no saliva formed. He glanced at his mama who was smiling reassuringly at him. His parents taught them to be honest and encouraged debate at home. It was okay to disagree at times but never okay to disobey. He didn't want to disagree with his mama in public.

"Tell us what you really think, son," said Jalisa, noticing his dilemma.

"Girls should be taught self-defense so that they can protect themselves when attacked. But most of the time they don't walk around with sticks so teaching them intonga would be pointless."

"It went well for your sister, didn't it?" said Marikana. "She is the reason we are here."

A murmur rippled through the audience prompting the Elder to raise his hand for silence.

"My sister was lucky; she was dealing with an inkwenkwe, a mama's boy. Someone more formidable might have posed a greater challenge but bullies are never that. But she had sticks because she was training during recess. That won't be the case if we decide to formally train girls at intonga. I don't always carry my sticks with me."

"So you oppose teaching intonga to girls?"

"Yes."

"The dinner conversation at the Matthews' household will be interesting tonight," said Marikana, and the crowd tittered. "The council will confer and we will have an answer in a few days. If there is no other business, we will dismiss."

No one spoke up, so the horn blew.

Chapter 15

When Tola entered Civics class on Monday, Mr. Kimani beckoned him over. As he approached his teacher, Tola noticed that Pumla was present.

"Tola, I am assigning you a new partner for your project. I'm sorry, but I'm not at liberty to explain why. Judge Molodi is your new partner. Why don't you catch him up on what you have so far?"

Mr. Kimani moved on to another student who needed his attention leaving Tola alone and perplexed. Tola and Judge weren't friends, but were friendly enough. Judge was more academic while Tola was more athletic. Although Judge was smart, he was also humble and willing to assist anyone in need.

But he was not the desire of Tola's heart. He wasn't Pumla. Tola could tell that Pumla was avoiding his gaze. What happened? he wondered.

"Alright, get to your seats, please," hollered Mr. Kimani.

Tola passed by Judge and they decided to have lunch to strategize. Tola resolved to find out from

Pumla why she ditched him. He had fought men and killed beasts; why was confronting Pumla so frightening?

Pumla sat alone at lunch which Tola recognised as a God-given opportunity. She was popular and rarely alone. She had her back to him which was also divine providence so she couldn't escape as he approached.

"Tola!"

Balisa's call not only caught Tola's attention but Pumla's as well. She turned and caught Tola's eye. He thought she would quickly turn away, but she didn't. They connected for a few seconds, then with a small smile, she gestured for him to come over.

"Please sit down," she said. "I owe you an explanation."

Tola sat across from her.

"Your sister hurt my brother."

"What?"

"You know what I'm talking about," said Pumla. "My mother visited your family and showed you what your sister did."

Tola's eyes saucered as the realization dawned on him.

"Terence is your brother."

"You didn't know?"

"Did you know that Lindi was my sister?"

"Touche."

Tola waited for her to continue.

"My mama found out that you were my project partner and demanded that I get another one."

"Do you always do what your mama tells you?"

"Yes," responded Pumla.

Of course you do, Tola thought. He sighed. "I'm disappointed. We never really got started, and I was looking forward to working on the project with you."

"Hopefully, we'll have another opportunity," said Pumla.

Tola wanted to have his lunch with her but his friends were waiting.

"I'll see you around then," he said, getting up to leave.

After a couple of steps, he turned to her.

"By the way, I don't suppose you'll tell me who took our meat, will you?" he asked.

When she looked at him, he saw the conflict she was grappling with. It was clear that she knew who the thieves were but was unsure whether to reveal it.

"It's okay, Pumla," he said. "Stay well."

Then he joined his friends.

Chapter 16

Tola didn't feel up to attending football practice after school. It was the first practice of the season and the first game was next week against a major rival. Despite his reluctance, he showed up, but Mr. Kimani noticed his lacklustre engagement.

"What's going on, Tola?"

"I'm sorry, Coach," Tola replied. "There's something going on at home, and the partner switch with Pumla has me distracted. I thought I could get my head in the practice but I can't. Can I be excused?"

"We have a game next week, son," said Mr. Kimani. "We're going to go through some set plays today. I need you to concentrate, Tola. This isn't like you. Get back to your teammates."

Mr. Kimani was right. One of Tola's strengths was his ability to block everything out and concentrate on the task at hand. It was why he was able to excel at Intonga. During matches, he didn't hear the crowd. It was him and the opponent.

Pumla had him confused, Lindi had him concerned, and the theft left him unsettled. These were foreign feelings to him. He was used to being level-headed in all situations. Balisa and Zac had a way of keeping him calm but they weren't on the team; they preferred rugby and cricket respectively. John Bokwe, the team captain, was engaged in a motivational speech when Tola joined the huddle, which helped.

Practice ended around 5 pm. Tola declined several offers for rides home and decided to jog instead. The sun hung low behind him and a cool, gentle breeze was refreshing. Halfway home, a couple of cars passed him by. Most people would be at home enjoying supper by now. He quickened his pace, looking forward to whatever Mama had prepared. A fast moving car approached, driving in the centre of the two-lane road. As it came closer, Tola recognised the model as a Peugeot 504. He stopped, wanting to make out the driver. He didn't recognise him. However, he did recognise the scared boy, crying in the back seat: it was Pumla's brother, Terence.

Chapter 17

Tola was both surprised and unsurprised that Bwana was in his home when he burst in breathlessly. What truly surprised him was that Yoliswa was there as well. The two of them joined Jalisa around the kitchen table.

"I think Jogba and The Future are in the area," he blurted out.

"Why do you say that?" asked Bwana. "Did you see him?"

"I saw his car," said Tola. "I'll never forget that vehicle. But he wasn't driving-someone else was. And he had a familiar passenger in the back seat."

He paused, engaging in a habit he disliked when others did it. There was no need to wait for the next obvious question. Just spit it out!

"It was Terence," he said. "He looked terrified. I believe he's been kidnapped."

Bwana nodded slightly, as if he were not surprised by the news.

"So they are back in action," he said. "We need to warn all the village elders. Which village is Terence from?"

"Madiba," answered Tola. "We've become acquainted with the family. They're probably wondering where Terence is and don't know he's been kidnapped. Who's going to tell them?"

He could go, but it wasn't his responsibility. Women wailing over sad news was something he wasn't used to; it always unnerved him at funerals. He didn't know why.

"I'll send some men over there and the surrounding villages," said Bwana, rising from his seat. "In the meantime, I have to find Terence before they do anything to him."

Tola hesitated.

Then he said, "I'm coming with you."

"So am I," said Lindi, appearing from behind the sheet that marked her room. "It'll make up for what I did to Terence if I can help rescue him. Please!"

Bwana looked at Jalisa. He knew Lindi was out of the question, but he wasn't sure how she would feel about her son joining this dangerous mission. Jalisa reached out to her daughter and drew her to her side.

"Someday, little one," she said, "but not today." To her son, she said, "It is for moments like this that you were made. The battles, the hunts, the captures and escapes have prepared you to help your fellow man. This is your moment. Go with my blessing. Go with our God."

Chapter 18

"You two are here as observers," said Bwana.

Tola and Yoliswa exchanged glances and nodded in agreement with Bwana's announcement. The air-conditioned Land Rover sped toward the location indicated by the satellite images showing where The Future was. Since The Future never stayed in one place for long, time was of the essence.

Tola hoped they would arrive in time for Terence's sake. The boy had endured a rough couple of weeks, facing embarrassment at the hands of Lindi, and now being kidnapped. He kissed his two intonga sticks which gave him comfort; one bore the names of his parents, and the other, his siblings.

"Those sticks won't help you against bullets," Yoliswa said, amused.

Tola laughed. "They can't stop a bullet, but they're quite effective when the element of surprise is at play."

"Hopefully you've improved since our last battle. You made it easy for me."

"The last time we fought, I was drugged. When this is over, I'm up for another match."

"Okay, you two," said Bwana. "We'll be meeting up with other agents shortly and then taking a helicopter to the site. Local officers have the area surrounded and are waiting for our arrival. No one engages The Future until we get there. I need you to keep your wits about you. Are you ready?"

"Ready!"

They had to shout their response over the whirring rotors of the helicopter. They climbed in, joining two agents and four soldiers strapped into their seats.

Bwana mounted his headset. "Let's go, pilot!" he bellowed.

The aircraft lifted off. Tola exhaled.

Chapter 19

There was a good chance that The Future had lookouts so the approach of the helicopter would be noticed. Tola was impressed with its quietness and learned that it was a Eurocopter EC145, which was one of the quieter helicopters in its class. After fifteen minutes, they landed and rushed to the perimeter of the camp and met up with the team leader.

"Any movement?" asked Bwana.

Captain Sizwe pointed toward three young teen boys they had captured. They were seated on the ground and were guarded by a soldier.

"They were patrolling the area," he said. "They said some new recruits had arrived but they didn't know their names. Jogba is there. How do you want to handle this?"

"Is everyone in place?" asked Bwana.

"Yes," Sizwe replied. "Who's this?"

"This is Yoliswa and Tola. They are here as observers."

"We're bringing kids on dangerous missions now?" asked Sizwe.

"Are you questioning my decisions now?" retorted Bwana.

After a short staredown, Bwana said, "You two stay here. Be careful. Some men might flee this way. If they do, do not engage. Stay out of sight and let them go. Am I clear?"

"Yes, sir," said Yoliswa, and Tola nodded.

"Okay, let's go," said Bwana.

Bwana spoke into his walkie-talkie and the team moved forward. Tola watched until they were swallowed by the forest.

Chapter 20

In the excitement of the moment, Tola didn't notice how quickly darkness fell. The night was bright as the moon and the numerous stars shone brightly. There hadn't been much rain lately, so the humidity was low and the ground was dry.

The forest's nightlife was alive. Insects chirped, birds called out, and vines rustled as monkeys swung to and fro. The silence of slithering snakes and scampering spiders made Tola uneasy. A cluster of fireflies danced by before disappearing into the dense thicket.

Tola wanted to speak to the three prisoners. He felt sorry for what they must have endured but was elated that they were free from the devil, Jogba. They had to find Terence before any harm came to him. What was going on? he wondered.

"Are we going to stand here and do nothing?" asked Yoliswa, reading his mind.

Tola was reminded of when he asked Pumla if she always did what her mama said. She had unhesitatingly replied yes. Now someone for whom they had mutual respect had given them an order. Should he disobey?

"We are, for now," he answered. "Unlike you, I am one who respects authority. However, if a sign should come our way, I am not opposed to following it."

"What kind of sign?" asked Yoliswa.

"We'll know it when we see it."

"It had better show up quickly," said Yoliswa, "because I'm getting antsy."

Tola smiled and walked toward the three boys. Yoliswa didn't follow him. A firefly did. It flew in front of him and then landed on his shoulder. This was unusual as fireflies usually travelled in groups. Then it flew to his left, turned toward him, hovered, then took off again.

"Yoliswa!" Tola hollered.

"Yes," responded Yoliswa, running toward him.

"We have our sign," said Tola, and he followed the firefly.

Chapter 21

It was about a forty-five-second jog that the firefly led them on. The initial long grass they had to navigate shortened, making it easier to follow. Then it stopped, turned, and hovered. It disappeared into the night as if it had turned off its luminescence. Tola and Yoliswa surveyed their surroundings.

"Do you see anything?" asked Tola.

Yoliswa didn't get a chance to answer him. They heard a rustling sound that grew louder with every passing second.

"Get down," said Yoliswa.

From their crouched position they were able to see a man running frantically, looking over his shoulder in panic. He hurried past them when Tola recognized him and gasped.

"Jogba!" he called out after a couple of heartbeats.

Jogba spun around. In the bright moonlight, his gaze fixed on Tola as if he recognized him but couldn't remember where from. Tola said nothing as he unsheathed his intonga sticks.

"Tola," said Jogba, realization dawning on him. "You've grown up."

"That's what happens with time," said Tola.

"Indeed," said Jogba. "Is this your babysitter?"

Yoliswa moved to approach Jogba, but Tola put a stick out in front of her.

"He's mine," he said.

Jogba sneered. "Hand me one of your sticks and let's battle. If I win, you let me go. Deal?"

"No deal," said Yoliswa. "You have to answer for your crimes. You have kidnapped and drugged boys, murdered innocent villagers, and I can't imagine what you've done to women. There's no way we're letting you go. Right, Tola?"

Tola squeezed his sticks so hard that blood drained from his knuckles. His heart felt like a wartime drumbeat, and it felt like lava coursed through his veins. Yoliswa was saying something, but he heard nothing. His surroundings blurred. All he could see was Jogba in front of him. He released one stick and tossed it to Jogba.

"Deal," he said.

Chapter 22

Yoliswa turned to protest but when she looked into Tola's eyes, she stopped and stepped aside. The quiet of the African night was broken by the distant cackle of a hyena. The radiant moon spotlighted the battle zone, so much so that Tola almost missed a firefly hovering over Jogba for a moment then disappearing. That moment was his assurance that he made the right decision.

Jogba moved first. He came forward swinging, strikes whipping through the air, relentless and brutal. Tola blocked the first, ducked the second, but a third caught him across the ribs. Gasping, he staggered back, wincing in pain. Jogba encircled him laughing, twirling his stick expertly.

"You underestimated me, didn't you, Tola?" Jogba spat.

Maybe, thought Tola. He was surprised by Jogba's speed and agility. He was glad that it was evident early so he knew not to make that mistake again. He was also grateful that Jogba, in his arrogance, gave him a chance to catch his breath.

"You look like a man," Jogba taunted, "but you fight like a boy."

Jogba liked to attack so Tola decided to stand his ground. He didn't have to wait long. Jogba advanced. Tola didn't retreat. He met the next strike with a cross block, twisting at the last second and crashed his stick into Jogba's wrist. A crack echoed. Jogba grunted, stepping back, favoring the limb.

Tola moved in a blur, driving forward with new energy. He spun low, sweeping Jogba's leg with a snap of his stick. Jogba stumbled but didn't fall. Instead, he roared and launched a heavy, downward strike meant to end the fight. Tola sidestepped and delivered a devastating jab to Jogba's ribs. Jogba gasped. He then swung his stick at Jogba's shins causing him to fall to his knees. Then he struck him on the side of his head and he fell to the ground, not unconscious, but stunned and beaten.

Chapter 23

"Is everyone alright here?"

That question was asked by Bwana who appeared with two police officers. Surveying the scene, he saw Tola standing victoriously over Jogba. He approached him.

"You can breathe now, son," said Bwana. "You got him."

Tola wasn't aware that he had stopped breathing. Adrenaline still flooded his body and his head throbbed in beat with the thudding of his heart.

What?" he muttered.

Bwana relieved him of his stick and placed it in its sheath.

"It's over," said Bwana, placing a hand on Tola's shoulder. "Jogba will no longer be a problem thanks to you. He's going away for a long time." He gestured to the police officers. "Arrest this man and don't forget to read him his rights."

"Did you find Terence?" asked Tola, retrieving his other stick.

Bwana nodded in the affirmative. "He was scared but he's safe and sound. He's in the helicopter ready to be taken to the LandRover. I can drop you home first before taking Terence home if you prefer."

While Tola avoided informing the family of Terence's kidnapping, he relished returning him home. Sure, there will be tears but they will be tears of joy.

"No, I would like to be there when you return him home," he said.

Bwana smiled. "I thought you might. How about you, Yoliswa."

Yoliswa shook her head. "I'm going to run home from here. Shanla isn't too far and it's a nice night." She turned to Tola approvingly. "You did well. I look forward to our next battle. I think it will be a challenge this time."

"Thank you, my sister," said Tola.

He was starting to see her that way. In all honesty, he was happy she was there to back him up if he got into any trouble. Thankfully, she wasn't required. He might never have heard the end of it.

Chapter 24

The walk up to Pumla's front door took forever. Terence sprinted to it and squeals of elation ensued. No doubt tears flowed as well. The weight on Tola's feet was due to the unknown reaction to his presence.

They didn't know that he was part of the rescue and would initially wonder what he was doing there. How would that manifest? Anger? Disdain?

It was neither. Before he reached the door, Pumla rushed out and hugged him. With tears streaming down her face, she hung on long enough to show her appreciation. The hug she gave Bwana was shorter, Tola noted.

"Please, come in," said Aunt Gladys. She balanced Terence on her hip. "Sit down and celebrate with us."

There was no need for her to cook or bake anything as villagers had brought meals as a means of support. The village quickly heard of Terence's return and rejoiced with music and singing. It wasn't long before a couple of goats were killed to add to the feast. Some from other villages attended the festivities including Jalisa, who showed up with Lindi.

"Where's Nomsa?" asked Tola.

"Sleeping at Auntie J's," said Lindi. "How is Terence?"

Tola didn't need to respond as Terence and his mother approached them. Aunt Gladys' eyes moistened as she took Jalisa's hands in hers.

"I was so scared," she said, her lips trembling.

"I know exactly how you felt," said Jalisa, as they embraced.

Terence smiled at Lindi. "Do you think you could have rescued me like your brother did?" he said.

Tola marveled at the gracious spirit Terence had with that question. The physical scars had healed but emotional scars took longer to dissipate.

"Let's hope I never have to find out," said Lindi. Good answer.

Terence and Lindi ran off while Gladys took Jalisa to get something to eat. As Tola stood alone, he saw Pumla with a group of friends. They looked his way and giggled. Tola grunted inwardly and turned away to go somewhere. Anywhere.

"Tola!"

Tola heard his name called in stereo. Behind him, Pumla called. To his right, Bwana. Tola turned to acknowledge Pumla but Bwana won his attention.

"I'll be quick," said Bwana, with a wink. "I'm taking off. Tola, when the school year is over, I want you to spend a few weeks at Intelligence headquarters. We have internship programmes where we introduce qualified students to some of what we do. Talk to your parents, if you're interested."

"I'm interested," Tola blurted.

Bwana laughed. "Talk to your parents, young man," he repeated. "I'll keep in touch. Now, go and talk with that young lady."

Tola's mind was spinning with Bwana's proposal that he didn't notice Pumla arguing with two men.

Chapter 25

"Tola, this is Bhuti and Khumo," said Pumla.

"It's nice to meet you, Tola," said Khumo, outstretching his right hand. "We've heard a lot about you. You're impressive."

Tola shook his hand and then Bhuti's.

"Thank you," he said. He had a hunch. "Pumla told me that you stole my springbok meat. You should be brought to justice and I expect to be compensated for that theft."

"I don't know how he found out, but it wasn't me," cried Pumla, wide-eyed.

"Shut up," snapped Khumo.

It was too late. Tola's triumphant smile disappeared when he saw Pumla's realization that she had been tricked. She gazed at him with sadness and disappointment, and with moistening eyes turned and walked away. Tola wanted to go after her but he had to deal with Bhuti and Khumo first.

"So, it's true that you two stole my meat?" he asked.

Yes," said Khumo, and Bhuti agreed.

"How did you do it?"

They went on to confirm what Bwana had surmised. Tola listened, uninterrupting the narrative, and marvelling the smarts of his mentor.

"Was Terence the child you used in your escapade?" he asked.

Khumo and Bhuti shared a glance.

"We're going to let Pumla answer that question," said Bhuti.

Tola was sure he knew the answer.

"We're sorry," said Bhuti.

Tola sighed deeply. A special moment in this life was ruined by their act. He and his friends will go on another hunt but there will never be another first time. His mama and sister approached and announced that they were heading home.

"I'm coming with you," he said.

He walked past the two friends without a response to their apology. He wanted them to stew for a while. Lindi took his hand in hers and they shared a fond look. He will enjoy this for as long as he can. She's growing up so fast.

Epilogue

A month later, Tola, Balisa, and Zach prepared to go on their next hunting trip. At 5 am, they met at Tola's home to set off.

It had been an eventful month. First, the Inkatha justice system wasted no time in convicting and sentencing Jogba and The Future. Jogba was sentenced to life imprisonment with no chance of parole. His crimes against children were heinous and unforgivable, and the judge informed him that were the death penalty available, he would have received that. The charge of treason was dropped.

Second, Bhuti and Khumo were brought before the council of elders in their village. They pleaded guilty and anyone who ate of the meat had to pay restitution to the three friends. The payment could be in the form of money or livestock. Terence was considered an innocent participant but to learn his lesson, he had to clean the Ukopha every weekend for six months.

Tola and Judge got an A for their presentation on

the History of the Ilanga Provinces.

"Ready to go?" asked Zach.

"Yes, we are."

Zach and Balisa spun in the direction of the responder. It was Lindi and she was dressed for hunting. They simultaneously looked quizzically at Tola, who shrugged.

"I think she's ready to come with us, guys. Tata and Mama agree."

"Don't you think you should have talked to us first," said Zach.

"Would you have said no?" asked Tola.

"Probably not," replied Zach, "but that's not the point; it's the principle."

Balisa put his arm around Tola and took him aside.

"Is there anything else you want to go against tradition on, my friend," he asked.

Tola laughed and smiled at his little sister. "We're just getting started," he said.

Vuyo Ngcakani

Vuyo Ngcakani is a husband, father of three grown children, and proud grandfather of two. He lives in Nova Scotia with his wife, where family remains at the center of his life. Drawing from his upbringing in a large, close-knit family, and more than 25 years of teaching youth in church, he writes stories that highlight faith, courage, and responsibility.